Tumbuka Folktales

Moral and Didactic Lessons
from Malaŵi

Lester Brian Shaŵa
&
Boston Jaston Soko

Mzuni Publications
Mzuzu University
P/Bag 201
Luwinga
Mzuzu 2
Malaŵi

ISBN 99908-57-03-2

Illustrations by: Myke Mtika

Contents

Preface

This folklore collection is based on field research conducted by the authors in Citumbuka speaking areas of Mzimba and Rumphi districts in northern Malaŵi. It was observed that in most areas the folktale repertoire is dwindling, after some two to five stories, the respondents would find themselves dry, asking one another for help. It is apparent that the rural population is facing tremendous pressure to turn to modern ways of living. In this connection, oral literature is fast becoming an inefficient means of traditional education. This is inevitably leading to loss of the cultural heritage.

The effort of Messrs Lester Brian Shaŵa and Boston Soko in coming up with this collection of folktales is a result of their profound interest in their culture and desires to preserve their cultural patrimony. Two immediate uses of the collection could be highlighted. In the first place, the collection will be of great use as a textbook to the youth of Malaŵi, most of whom have no opportunity to participate in live folktale performances. In the second place, the collection will preserve some of the stories. The authors have collected the tales for all interested in cultural issues.

It is common knowledge today that people tend to look down upon folktales dubbed as literature for children. This is a misleading statement because unlike in the past, previous generations of the youth used to drink right from the source, that is to say, leading folktale tellers were elderly men and women whose interest was specifically to transmit wisdom to the younger generations besides providing amusement during sessions. In all this, the emphasis was on the respect for tradition as well as nature in general. The respect for tradition went along with the belief that everything, according to their vision of the world, trees, animals, rivers, stones, mountains, were endowed with life, hence the interaction between humans and non-humans in the folktales. Mountains, trees or stones were believed to be the abode of the spirits. Because today respect for these has disappeared, we see the wanton cutting down of trees, the destruction of sacred places and the disinterest in oral traditions. To reiterate what has been said by many illustrious people; a nation without culture is worthless.

In conclusion, I wish to state that part of Mzuzu University's mission is to embark on projects intended to rehabilitate the Malaŵian cultural patrimony, thus the Research and Publications Committee should be commended for funding projects in the domain of Oral Literature. The collections may well serve as reference books in libraries and this is the only way folktales could be preserved in Malaŵi.

Prof. Boston Jaston Soko, Mzuzu University, October 2005

Acknowledgements

Foremost, we are grateful to the Mzuzu University Research and Publications Committee under the Directorate of Professor Heyden Boyd for funding the research that has culminated into this collection. His successor, the Assistant Director of Research, Mr. Joel Luhanga deserves special mention for all his assistance and suggestions. We are also thankful to the current Director of Research, Dr. O.V. Msiska for his pertinent guidance.

We are indebted to all informants who narrated folktales in Mzimba and Rumphi districts in the northern region of Malaŵi. We acknowledge the following people who assisted in organising groups of informants: Mr and Mrs Nkhombo Banda, Village Headman (VH) Xema, Mr. Chaphonya Banda, Mr. Kadoko Hara, Mrs. Zuwayumo, Mr. I.G. Chiromo, Group Village Headmen (GVH) Kamzinga Mkandawire and Vyalema Nyirongo and Senior Group Village Headman (SGVH) Kaiwale.

Professor Fr. John Ryan was the project mentor and he contributed greatly to the success of this collection.

In a special way, we register our profound gratitude to Professor Pascal Kishindo for editing this collection.

Further, we would like to thank Mr. M. Chaura and Mrs. Monique Mwalwanda for video-taping folktale performances and assisting in transcribing the collection respectively.

All colleagues numerous to mention who encouraged us to research and eventually come up with this collection are sincerely acknowledged.

Lester Brian Shaŵa & Prof. Boston Jaston Soko, Mzuzu University, October 2005

Dedicated to Lester's mother, Theresa Kanyasko, who narrated and
performed folktales with passion.

Prologue

Kukhumbikwa kwa Midauko ya Citumbuka

Tikuwonga kwiza kwa mwaŵalendo, tawonga
Palije aŵo ŵalikutenderapo nga ndimwe, tawonga
Kuti ŵatichiske mu ukhaliro withu, tawonga

Tikuwonga fumu yithu Kamzinga, tawonga
Cifukwa ca kuzomerezga ŵalendo aŵa, tawonga
Ŵalendo aŵa mbakuzirwa comene, tawonga
Yewo mwaŵalendo na vya kuzirwa ivi, tawonga
Ŵana ŵithu ŵasambire makora, tawonga
Lutirilani kutichiska, tawonga

Ŵana ŵithu ŵasambile midauko
Vidokoni na nthalika nazo tichitenge
Magule ghithu gha Citumbuka tivinenge

Ŵana ŵithu ŵakule na nkharo yiweme, tawonga
Taŵapapi tiŵasambizge nkharo yiweme, tawonga
Ŵana ŵithu nawo ŵakule makora, tawonga
Mwaŵalendo, mwizeso, tawonga

Mwaŵalendo ka mukaŵankhuni nyengo yose iyi?

Recited by Jane Mwase, Bolero, Rumphi, 2 May 2005

The need for Tumbuka Heritage

We are grateful for the visit, we thank you
No one has visited us like you, we thank you
To enlighten us on our heritage, we thank you

We are thankful to Kamzinga our chief, we thank you
For accepting our visitors, we thank you
These visitors are very important, we thank you
Thanks visitors for these important issues, we thank you

Our children should cherish our heritage
Let us tell folktales and riddle
Let us dance to our Tumbuka dances

Our children should have proper upbringing, we thank you
We need to teach our children good manners, we thank you
Our children should have proper upbringing, we thank you
Visitors you should come again, we thank you

Visitors, where were you all this time?

*Translated by Lester Brian Shawa, Mzuzu University,
October 2005*

Introduction

The East African writers Ngugi Wa Thiong'o, Taban Lo Liyong and Awuor Anyumba in a joint statement argue that the best way to reintroduce the African Man into the world must be first to reintroduce him to himself and his environment (Singano & Roscoe, 1974). Without a cultural background to lean on, a person lacks necessary support to engage with education meaningfully. People, who lack proper cultural background, remain foreigners to themselves.

In Malaŵi, like in many other African countries, very little has been written on Oral Literature. During my undergraduate studies, I worked on a project that assessed the relevance of Tumbuka Oral Literature in the modern Malaŵi. Basically, I collected songs, riddles, proverbs, and figurative sayings and analysed themes inherent in relation to our life today. This collection is a result of further research stemming from my previous work and interest.

The idea of the collection is to contribute to the preservation of Tumbuka cultural heritage that has seriously suffered from proper transmission in the recent years owing to several reasons. The following two being most pertinent: firstly, most elderly people (the guardians of wisdom) among the Tumbuka people have died leaving a generation that is almost ignorant of their cultural heritage. Secondly and most prominent, very little has been recorded on Tumbuka cultural heritage.

Tumbuka folktales are on the verge of extinction. If not recorded now, the loss would not only be the amusement they provide but chiefly lessons inherent. On the surface, they are simple narratives, however, subtly they evoke serious moral lessons that are very applicable to our everyday life today... only if we listened.

Sources

The authors used primary sources by collecting information from talented men and women in folktale narrative performance from Rumphi and Mzimba districts in the northern region of Malaŵi. The narrated folktales were tape-recorded, transcribed and translated into English. Preparatory visits to organise informants in Rumphi district were done from 14 March to 16 March, 2005 while official tape-recordings were done from 30 April to 5 May 2005. Preparatory visits to organise informants in Mzimba district were done from 3 April to 7 April, 2005 while official tape-recordings were done on 5 May, and then from 17 May to 25 May, 2005. The following picture shows authors collecting information from narrators.

Shaŵa in white shirt facing camera and Soko also in white shirt with back to the wall

The exercise was not easy since most people have forgotten folktales told by elders. Hence, it was not surprising that in most cases narrators only remembered songs that accompany the tales. However, since we travelled extensively a substantial amount of tales was collected.

The most exciting part nevertheless, was the zeal, the interest and the love shown by the villagers as they narrated folktales. The importance they attached to the exercise was very vivid. For example, at Kamzinga Village (Bolero, Rumphi) while recording folktales, one lady, Jane Mwase interrupted and asked us to listen to her *leketulo* (poem). Amazingly what followed was a beautiful poem on the importance of Tumbuka cultural heritage and great appreciation to us for trying to revive it. This clearly revealed that people would like lessons taught by parents to flourish and be used as basis for preserving their heritage. The poem forms the prologue to this collection.

Themes/Topics

A theme of a work is its central idea which may be stated directly or indirectly (Cuddon, 1991). The tales have been grouped into themes or topics, which are moralistic and/or didactic in nature. The grouping of the tales into themes is not supposed to be rigid. It only exemplifies lessons inherent in Tumbuka folktales. Of course this collection cannot in any way exhaust all the lessons. The tales fall under the following topics: *Observing and Explaining Creation, Fertility, Marriage Counselling, Care for Orphans, Good Behaviour, Warning against Beasts, Respect for Elders and Tricksters*. Each theme is introduced before the tales. The introductions analyse the topics and show their relevance to modern society. Questions are asked after each and every story to tickle thinking and application to modern life.

Problems of translations

Without question, it is difficult to translate Tumbuka folktales into English and retain the same level of meaning. Perhaps the most difficult part in translating Tumbuka folktales into English, are the songs that accompany and complement the tales. Indeed, some explanations may not be narrated but simply sung. Thus songs play a pivotal role during a folktale performance. The rhythms produced also add to the imagination as one listens to a folktale narration. Unfortunately, this is impossible to reproduce when folktales are written down. With these challenges in mind however, in this collection, the songs are kept in Tumbuka and translated into English. Expectedly, the translations in most cases have been made literally to try to grasp the original meaning.

The structure of Tumbuka folktales

Tumbuka folktales depend on the narrator and the audience that, from time to time, responds to the leader. The leader is the main performer and the way he/she performs affects the quality (in terms of amusement) of the folktale. He leads in the gestures and the songs that accompany the tale. The songs are mostly repeated since they complement the tale. This is why in this collection songs that accompany tales are repeated so as to come closer to the performed versions. Sometimes the songs are onomatopoeic in nature and the leader vividly illustrates this through the sounds. The line below exemplifies this:

> "Baa baa yalira ng'ombe ya Nya Banda"
> (Literally translated: Baa baa the cow of Mrs Banda has cried),
> where baa describes the moo of a cow.

Setting in Tumbuka folktales

Tumbuka folktales have varied settings. Settings may be villages, bushes, crop gardens, wells, and other places.

In Malaŵi, most Tumbuka-speaking people starting about early 1920s went to work in the mines in South Africa, Zimbabwe or Zambia. These places have also given settings to several folktales. For example, folktales depicting life in these places, people killing each other or losing luggage on their way to Malaŵi or, indeed, being eaten by animals have been told. The tales were, however, usually told in very imaginative manner with serious lessons behind them.

Characterisation in Tumbuka folktales

Characters are mostly human beings, animals, plants or vegetables, supernatural beings and others. In most tales, animals are personified (given human qualities). Through characterisation, the superstitious nature of the Tumbuka community is revealed. For example, in one folktale a man drank all the water from a well to compel the snake that had swallowed his wife and daughter to vomit them alive.

Target group

This collection targets several people. For those who would like just to enjoy reading the tales, they will find the collection very interesting. For those interested in cultural issues, here is a collection of a rich cultural heritage that explains a people's aspirations and identity. For teachers of Oral Literature, here is a collection that can be used to explain several literary devices like themes, plots, setting and characterisation while simultaneously improving students' reading, vocabulary, sentence construction and comprehension. A model lesson plan has been made available for teachers.

In the main, people will appreciate lessons society has taught from generation to generation. These lessons are relevant today hence it is vital to see them in relation to our own modern society.

Lester Brian Shaŵa, Mzuzu University, October 2005

CHAPTER ONE

Observing and Explaining Creation

"Look, why does the tortoise have a scarred shell?"

INTRODUCTION

The Tumbuka people just like most ethnic groups, have used folktales to explain what they observe and see around their environment. Folktales have been used to explain creation especially where there are no obvious answers. By explaining what they observe and see, they reveal their awareness to the surroundings and their quest to know. It is natural for humanity to desire or want to know.

Most of these simple explanations have been answers to children's questions such as, where does the rain come from? Where do children come from? Why does a leopard have beautiful spots? And so on. These are the most basic type of folktales and are important in as far as they reveal what people experience in their environment, which usually has serious impact on their beliefs, customs and their way of life in general.

1
LION AND TITI THE BIRD

Once upon a time, Lion and Titi the bird were very good friends. Unfortunately, since Titi the bird is tiny he could only manage to kill and eat small insects and starved most of the time. Naturally, Lion did not like his friend to starve.

"Why do you keep eating these small insects?" asked Lion.
"It's because I cannot manage to kill the big ones, I am really starving", said the little bird.

Lion then decided to give his friend some medicine in order to transform him into a bigger animal. After the medicine, the little bird changed into a cat. Contentedly now he could manage to catch bigger animals. Seeing that as a cat Titi was well behaved the lion decided to fetch more medicine for him to become bigger than a cat. Well done now he became a leopard. Joyfully, the leopard caught stronger animals and enjoyed his killing. Convinced that the leopard was not pompous, Lion thought of transforming him into a lion, too. So he gave him some more medicine that he really became a fierce lion.

> "Now that you are like me, whenever you kill an animal do not claim that you are the one who has killed it," said Lion.
> "What should I say then?" asked Titi the lion.
> *Ncane yayi, ndine yayi nakoma*" (It's not mine, it's not me who has killed it)

Titi the lion agreed. Indeed, every time he attacked and killed animals he would shout *Ncane yayi, ndine yayi nakoma* (It's not mine, it's not me who has killed it) then immediately, the lion would come and eat some of the meat. The friendship truly prospered.

One day, Titi the lion killed a buffalo. This time around, tired of singing for the lion that usually did not share with him his kill he shouted differently *Ncane ncane, ndine nakoma* (It's mine; it's mine I am the one who has killed it). Instantly, upon hearing this, lion appeared and angrily asked,

> "Why are you not thankful, why did you not call me as usual?"
> "You do not share with me your kill why should I?" answered Titi the lion.

Miserably, Lion got hold of Titi the lion and removed his powers from him and straight away Titi the lion became a bird again. Poor Titi the bird still eats small insects today.

Questions
1. Explain how Titi the bird managed to kill big animals.
2. Why was Lion angry at Titi the bird?
3. In our everyday life, do similar things happen? Give examples.
4. Explain how characters have been personified in this folktale.

2
HOW A LEOPARD GOT BEAUTIFUL SPOTS

One day, tortoise was busy eating *manda*, mushroom, in the bush and an elephant which was strolling around came to him.

"Good afternoon Mr. Elephant", greeted the tortoise.
"Good afternoon to you", replied the elephant.
"Where are you going, Mr. Elephant?" asked the tortoise.
"Have I asked you for the way?" shouted the elephant rudely. "I will now put you on top of the tree", he continued.

After putting the tortoise on top of the tree, the elephant left contentedly.

At the top of the tree the tortoise was very worried. How would he climb down on his own? He wondered. He waited for a long time for somebody to rescue him. As he was worrying, a hyena appeared.

"How are you Mr. Hyena?" greeted the tortoise from the tree.
"I am fine, but what are you doing in the tree?" asked the hyena.
"The elephant put me here, please would you take me down", pleaded the tortoise.
"Aaah! Am I the one who put you there", hyena said while laughing loudly.

The hyena went away in that manner. Later a leopard came and tortoise was still hoping to be rescued.

"How are you Mr. Leopard?" greeted the tortoise.
"I am fine, but what are you doing in the tree?" asked the leopard.
"The elephant put me here, please would you take me down", pleaded the tortoise.
"Well I will assist you", the leopard responded happily.

Quickly, the leopard climbed up the tree and rescued the tortoise. The leopard admired the tortoise's looks.

"You have very nice spots, but if they were black and white they would have been even better", said the leopard.

"I keep them like this deliberately but if you want some I will share with you and colour them as you wish", said the tortoise. He then asked the leopard to stretch his legs while he was fixing the spots and colouring them white and black and joyfully singing: *Munyako wakuti kawemi naweso kawemi* (If one does you good you must also do him good). In the end the leopard was grateful as he looked very beautiful and so he left happy. On his way he met the hyena who was surprised at the leopard's newly acquired beauty.

"Who has made you look beautiful, Mr. Leopard?" asked hyena

"It's the tortoise", answered the leopard.

Without listening further the hyena hurried to look for tortoise whom he found on his way home.

"Mr. Tortoise, my friend, please make me look like Mr. Leopard", he said.

"Fine, come along dear", responded the tortoise with a coarse voice.

The tortoise asked the hyena to stretch his legs while he was fixing the spots and colouring them awkwardly and singing: *Munyako wakuti kaheni naweso kaheni* (If one does you bad you must also do him bad). Fortunately, up to now the hyena has dull spots while the leopard has very beautiful ones.

Questions

1. Why did the elephant put the tortoise in the tree?
2. Explain how the leopard got white and black spots.
3. What other theme/s do you find in this folktale?
4. Describe the behaviour of the animals in the story.
5. How does this folktale teach people today about good behaviour?

3
WHY LIONS ATTACK PEOPLE ONLY WHEN THEY ARE CLOSE

Once upon a time, a man befriended a lion. They used to do everything together. One day, while walking in a bush, they saw a herd of buffaloes feeding.

"Let us kill one buffalo", said the man.
"That will be good meat," replied the lion.

Without delay, the man took his gun and shot down one buffalo. As friends they enjoyed the meat together. However, the lion was very surprised at the art of the man. He did not understand how one could just touch a stick and manage to kill a very strong animal in seconds.

Well, the next day they also went hunting in the bush and the man rested his gun on the right shoulder as usual. Suddenly the man fell down and cried,

"Please, please help me; remove the thorn under my foot"

The lion removed the thorn that had deeply pierced the man's foot.

"Aaah, now I am fine", said the man.

The lion wondered how the same man who from a far killed a buffalo just by a trigger could easily be beaten by something very close to him. Since then lions have never dared to attack people from afar. They only attack people at close quarters.

Questions
1. Who are the characters in the folktale?
2. Explain how the man killed a buffalo?
3. According to the story, why do lions only attack people at close quarters?

4
BIRDS' FEAST

Once upon a time, birds organised a feast. The chief bird told all the other birds that the feast would take place in the sky and advised all of them to strengthen their wings in order to fly properly to the venue.

The crow shared the news with his friend, tortoise, who salivated just upon hearing the news and pleaded with the crow to take him to the feast.

> "My friend, the feast is only for birds," said the crow.
> "Please make me look like you and carry me to the sky," insisted the tortoise.

The crow, therefore, made fake wings for tortoise and put feathers on his body in order to make it look like a bird. On the day of the feast, the crow carried his friend tortoise who pretended to be a bird. When they arrived, the chief bird gave a moving speech while they were all seated. Soon after the speech some birds started preparing appetising food. Mr. Tortoise was by now salivating profusely.

Later, the chief bird suggested that to show their greatness, all the birds should fly one by one with food to another venue in the sky. Suddenly Mr. Tortoise's face changed. How would he fly on his own? He wondered. Sensing danger, Mr. Tortoise called his friend crow and begged him to go to his wife and tell her to prepare a soft place for him to land on from the sky. The wife was to place all the mattresses on the spot so that tortoise could not injure himself.

Instantly, the crow flew to Mr. Tortoise's home and told his wife to prepare a place for the husband to land on. He maliciously told Mrs. Tortoise that the place must be very hard for the husband would be full after the party. Happy with the news, Mrs. Tortoise collected all the hardest rocks around the home and placed them where Mr. Tortoise would land on.

After overseeing the preparations, the crow flew back to the sky and told Mr. Tortoise to quietly throw himself down to avoid embarrassing himself at the feast while showing him the special place his wife had prepared for him to land on. Without hesitation, Mr. Tortoise threw himself down from the sky and landed himself on the rocks. Feeling pain he cried loudly,

"Why did you make the place so hard, my dear wife?"
"This is what your friend told me," answered the wife sorrowfully.

Mrs. Tortoise regretfully picked her husband up and took him to the house. Since that time, the tortoise has a scarred shell.

Questions
1. What is the relevance of this folktale today?
2. How is friendship portrayed in the folktale?
3. Do you have friends who behave like the crow? Share your experiences.

5
WHY DOGS DO NOT HAVE HORNS

Once upon a time, there lived a very prosperous man at Mcekaceka village. He reared a lot of animals such that kraals of goats, pigs, cattle surrounded the house. As a great man of the village he also kept dogs around the house.

In those days, dogs were like goats so they also had horns. However, the two animals did not like each other as each one of them wanted to show superiority over the other.

One day the dog said to the goat,

> "Do you know that I am more important than you at this compound?"
> "Why do you cheat yourself Mr. Dog?" said the goat.
> "Don't you know that the master always calls me first whenever he comes here?" said the dog.
> "Perhaps you also do not know that I protect all of you at night?" continued the dog.
> "Well, but do you know that whenever the master receives visitors he kills some of us to feed them?" replied the goat.

The quarrel continued for a long time until one day the two started fighting ferociously. Since the dog was born a fighter, he quickly took a stone and hit the goat into the mouth destroying some teeth in the process. Angrily, the goat took a stick and struck the dog's horns knocking them off. There was now a loud howling, so people quickly came and brought peace between the two. Unfortunately since that time dogs have never grown horns again and goats have some teeth missing.

Questions
1. Explain why the characters did not like each other in this folktale.
2. Why according to the story, do dogs not have horns?
3. Discuss why you think this story was told.

6
LIZARD, CHAMELEON AND DEATH

Before death engulfed humanity, two old people were holding the earth one at the sunrise and the other at the sunset so that people would not die. But this was too much work so they decided to send messages that would be binding as far as life and death were concerned to the rest of the people.

The old men were to send messages through chameleon and lizard. The old man who was holding the earth at the sunrise called chameleon and told him to go and tell people that they would not die but live forever while the one at the sunset called a lizard and told him to tell people that they would die.

The race started from far; chameleon from sunrise and lizard from sunset and people were anxiously waiting to receive the messages. The first message received was going to be binding. After a long time, people started to see some animal coming close to them. They wondered what message was going to come. Perspiring profusely, the lizard appeared first as people restlessly wanted to hear the message he had carried for them. The lizard raised his head, looked at the people sorrowfully and broke the sad news that people would die. People were very sad at the news and wondered whether the lizard was telling the truth. In their disbelief they waited to hear what message the chameleon was to bring to them. Some days passed but the chameleon was nowhere to be seen. Finally, when people almost gave up hope, the chameleon arrived, tired but smiling. When people asked what message he had carried for them the chameleon said that he had brought them good news that people would never die but live forever.

"But why did you not come at the right time?" people asked furiously.

"Do you mean that the lizard has already arrived?" asked chameleon.

Left with nothing to say, one by one people left the place downcast for they knew that they could not change anything. The truth was simple and clear that people would never live forever.

Questions

1. What characteristics do the animals mentioned in this folktale have?
2. Why did elders tell this folktale?
3. Explain why you think human beings die?
4. Write an essay entitled, "How my religion depicts death"

"People who lack proper cultural background remain foreigners to themselves"

CHAPTER TWO
Fertility

"Ŵasing'anga help me, I want a child"

INTRODUCTION

In Tumbuka society failure to have children is regarded as a very serious problem. Since Tumbuka society is patrilineal the problem is compounded when it is the woman who is infertile. In such cases men usually divorce their wives for other women. Thus infertile women are usually ridiculed hence they tend to take several measures to become productive such as using traditional medicine from traditional healers.

Lack of children translates into failure to continue the family lineage. Thus couples without children fail to affirm themselves in society. However, it is infertile women that suffer more from inferiority complex hence most fertility tales in Tumbuka reveal the pain and stigma that these women face. These tales, therefore, express sombre moods while depicting diverse ways that infertile women take in trying to be productive.

1
A COUPLE WITHOUT A CHILD

Once upon a time, there was a couple that stayed for a long time without having a child. Rumours about them as failures abounded in the whole village. Indeed, wherever they went even young people laughed at them. After being ridiculed for a long time they decided to consult a traditional healer to heal their infertility.

Upon reaching the traditional healer's place a tall, fierce looking wrinkled man came out of his hut and in a hoarse voice shouted,

"Your problem has been solved! You will have children; I am Catonda the greatest healer".

It was said that even villages from far away had heard about the eminence of this man. The couple wondered how without telling him their problem he had already known about it. They agreed he must be the greatest. Naturally they trembled before the greatest man.

Rising from where he sat, the fierce wrinkled man went into his hut and after a short time emerged with eight identical sticks and in his usual hoarse voice said,

> "Take these sticks and put them in a tightly covered clay pot for eight days".
> "Whatever you say we will do", the couple chorused.

After eight days, they carefully opened the clay pot and to their disbelief they found four female children in the pot one of whom was lame. Obviously the couple was very glad. They named the lame child Ncawaka, meaning, "It's for nothing".

With time all the three children married except Ncawaka who with her disability stayed close to her mother at home. Like any other child she liked visiting and sharing stories with her peers.

One morning Ncawaka's mother was going to farm far way from the village so she called aloud,

> "Ncawaka, Ncawakaaa, Ncawaka eeh!"
> "I am coming mum", she said while running towards her mother.
> "I am going to farm far away, please boil the beans and attend to them".
> "Yes mum, I shall do as advised", Ncawaka answered.

Ncawaka, therefore, stayed behind and prepared a fireplace on which she placed a clay pot full of red dry beans. For some time she attended to the boiling beans and kept adding firewood. But since dry beans take time to cook she slowly started losing concentration such that when her friends came to visit her she totally forgot her responsibility.

Meanwhile the beans boiled and boiled absorbing as much water as possible. It was not long before her friends started sniffing a smell of burnt beans.

"Are you cooking beans?" asked one of the visitors.

"Oh yes! I forgot to attend to them", answered a concerned Ncawaka.

She rushed to the fireplace and indeed the red beans now looked more or less like charcoal. While figuring out what to say to her mother she heard a loud voice calling,

"Ncawaka, Ncawakaaa, Ncawaka eeh!

"Yes mum, here I am", answered a worried Ncawaka.

"I can clearly smell burnt beans, what happened?" asked her angry mother.

"Well I am sorry, I was busy with friends", said Ncawaka regretfully.

"Yes, now I can see this is the problem with children from wood", shouted the mother.

"Oh, so I am not real, I am from wood!" cried Ncawaka.

To express her disappointment with her mother's remark, Ncawaka started singing:

Leader:	Mbuya
All:	Amama ŵanena
Leader:	Mbuya
All:	Amama ŵanena nili mwana wa msongolo
Leader:	Ivyo
All:	Ŵanena ivyo
Leader:	Ivyo
All:	Ŵanena ivyo nili mwana wa msongolo

Grand mother
My mother has said
Grand mother
My mother has said that I am a child from medicine
What she has said
What she has said is that I am a child from medicine.

After crying and singing tirelessly one of her elder sisters Tapiwa, meaning, "Given by God", appeared and found her crying and singing unstoppably.

"Why are you crying sister?" she asked.
"Our mother has said that I am not real, but I am from medicine", she answered.

Without delay, the elder sister also started howling:

Leader:	Mbuya
All:	Amama ŵanena
Leader:	Mbuya
All:	Amama ŵanena nili mwana wa msongolo
Leader:	Ivyo
All:	Ŵanena ivyo
Leader:	Ivyo
All:	Ŵanena ivyo nili mwana wa msongolo

Grand mother
My mother has said
Grand mother
My mother has said that I am a child from medicine
What she has said
What she has said is that I am a child from medicine.

The singing got louder and louder and it started to attract villagers. Suddenly another sister, Nthembozawo, meaning, "Their Curses", came and also wondered why her sisters were crying.

"Why are you crying sisters?" she asked.
"Our mother has said that we are not real, but we are from medicine", they chorused.
"So we are not real I am very disappointed", she said.

Immediately she also joined in the crying and singing. The noise was now unbearable. The fourth sister, Tamala, meaning, "We are finished" also came and ultimately all the children joined together in wailing and singing. At last they decided to return to their original state, so they became sticks again.

Questions

1. What does this folktale tell us about failure to have children in marriage among the Tumbuka?
2. Discuss what happens when married people fail to have children in your society.
3. Write an essay on: Problems of Infertility in African Cultures. (Use your personal experiences and other references where possible).
4. Why do you think the Tumbuka place so much value on having children?

2
A WOMAN CRYING FOR A CHILD

Once upon a time, in a big village, lived a couple that desperately wanted to have children. People in the village started to wonder as to what was the couple's problem. As usual the man constantly blamed his wife for the situation.

The wife had taken enough abuse from fellow women who kept murmuring each time she passed them in a group. One day she decided to consult a medicine man to find out what the problem was and indeed who among the two of them was the culprit.

The medicine man was a lean, soft spoken man with his teeth protruding on the sides of the mouth. Indeed when he talked one could see the teeth moving up and down as saliva spluttered onto his clients.

"Please assist me, we are failing to have children in the house, I would like to know who between us is barren", said the woman.
"I knew your problem before you came, the problem is with your husband but if you bring him here, I, the real medicine man, will heal your mediocre man", said the medicine man.
"But how can I convince him to come here?" asked the woman trembling.
"Woman! You will know yourself how to tell him, that is your problem", retorted the medicine man.

The woman was frightened and kept quiet.

"Please go and tell your husband and bring him here for a concoction", he continued.

The woman returned home. But culturally it was very difficult for her to tell her husband about the ordeal. What would he think about her? Who sent her? Some clandestine relationship with the medicine man perhaps? She could not find answers to these questions that she expected from her husband. She stayed for several days without a proper plan. One day she cleverly decided to tell the husband about the problem through song:

Mama ine eee mama ine eee
Bulangete mu nyumba mulije
Mama ine eee mama ine eee
Bulangete mu nyumba mulije

Ine nizgokere uku kuli cibowo,
Niti ntheura kuli cibowo
Cibowo calutilira mwawanalume wane
Bulangete munyumba mulije

Mama ine eee mama ine eee
Bulangete mu nyumba mulije
Mama ine eee mama ine eee
Bulangete mu nyumba mulije

Bulangeti ili ndimwe asweni wane
Bulangeti mu nyumba mulije
Ine nizgokere uku kuli cibowo
Niti ntheura kuli cibowo
Cibowo calutilira mwawanalume wane
Bulangete mu nyumba mulije

There is no blanket in the house
There is no blanket in the house
If I turn this way there is a hole
This way there is a hole
The hole has become a way of life
There is no blanket in this house.
This hole I mean you my husband

The husband did not comment quickly but he knew that the missing blanket had to do with him. He clearly knew that the blanket meant a child. Could it have been that she thinks the problem was his? The thoughts bothered him. However, the woman kept singing the piercing song.

Tired of listening to the song that pierced his heart the husband decided to ask his wife what she meant by the song. Thorny as it was she still explained to him about her ordeal. As expected her husband was very angry but fortunately after persuasion he accepted to accompany his wife to the doctor. Upon arrival the soft spoken lean doctor said,

"Your problem is now over"

Indeed saliva spluttered on the two as they looked at each other. The doctor prepared a concoction for them that they carried home. The man had to take prescribed measures of the concoction three times a day: in the morning, at lunch time and just before going to bed. After a considerable time, the woman conceived and bore a son that they happily named, Muzgezge, meaning, "Shadow".

Questions
1. Do you think infertility can be healed using traditional medicine today? Explain your answer with examples where possible.
2. Explain why most patrilineal societies in Africa stress on the need to have children in marriage.
3. Discuss why the woman decided to convey her plight through song.

"….it is infertile women that suffer more from inferiority complex hence most fertility tales in Tumbuka reveal the pain and stigma that these women face"

CHAPTER THREE

Marriage Counselling

"You are now a married woman. Please respect and take care of your husband"

INTRODUCTION

Marriage is very central among the Tumbuka patrilineal society as it unites two families and brings new relationships. For a Tumbuka marriage to last, good (accepted) behaviour is overriding. For instance, a well-behaved woman is well accepted at the husband's home where she belongs after marriage. Culturally, the newly married woman ought to understand how people behave in her new family thus she is initiated by elderly women on the accepted behaviour such as how to welcome visitors, how to take care of the husband, general cleanliness and other pertinent issues. The term used to describe this activity is kulanga, to teach or advise. Unfortunately, most marriages today do not last since marriage is mostly seen as a useless companionship that can be broken any time.

Among the Tumbuka the elders, through folktales, taught society on general marriage counsel for marriages to last. Perhaps it is pertinent to turn to these lessons now.

1
CHIEF AND HIS DAUGHTERS-IN-LAW

In a village long, long ago, there lived a chief with ten daughters-in-law. He enjoyed hunting and used to keep animal meat of different kinds in his hut. Every night he would share some of the meat with his daughters-in-law.

One of the daughters-in-law however, contrary to the village etiquette, used to secretly steal some of the meat from the chief's hut. The chief noticed this so he decided to call his daughters-in-law and said,

"I notice that someone is stealing some of the meat from my hut".
"That is unbelievable your honour", chorused the daughters-in-law.

Well, the next day the chief slaughtered a fat dog and cooked its tender meat which he kept in his hut as usual. It is hard to change some habits, so the thief secretly went to steal some meat from the chief's hut. Although she did not know it was dog meat, she still found it very tasty so she finished the whole of it.

When the chief came home, he noticed that somebody had eaten his tender meat. Tired of the unbelievable habit, he called all the daughters-in-law again.

"Daughters let us go to the river", he said, seeming strong and unmoved.
"Beautiful", they answered, "May be he wants to see how we draw water", they murmured amongst themselves.

When they arrived there, the chief tied a rope across the river.

"Will you cross the river one by one to the other side on the rope please?" said the chief in a strong tone of voice.

Silence and uncertainty engulfed the daughters. Terrified, they one by one started crossing to the other side of the river. While they were crossing, they were singing the following song:

Leader:	Warya garu ya fumu ni njani dungulira tera tera
All:	Dungulira tera tera
Leader:	Kwali mba kwali kwawo
All:	Dungulira tera tera

Who has eaten the chief's dog meat?
We do not know who
May be we do not know where she comes from

They all managed to do so up to the other side of the river. The chief asked them again to reveal if any one among them was responsible.

"That is unbelievable your honour", they chorused again.
"I give you the last chance; please may the one concerned reveal herself", he said furiously.

No one accepted responsibility. The chief commanded them to cross to the other side where they came from. While crossing the river, they continued singing their song:

Leader:	Warya garu ya fumu ni njani dungulira tera tera
All:	Dungulira tera tera
Leader:	Kwali mba kwali kwawo
All:	Dungulira tera tera

Who has eaten the chief's dog meat?
We do not know who
May be we do not know where she comes from

When nine daughters-in-law crossed successfully to the other side again only one remained. She started singing confidently while others were listening as she balanced on a rope.

"Daughter, if you are the one", said the chief in a tremulous voice, "please let me know."

"I do not eat dog meat, your honour", she answered confidently.

She continued singing:

Leader:	Warya garu ya fumu ni njani dungulira tera tera
All:	Dungulira tera tera
Leader:	Kwali mba kwali kwawo
All:	Dungulira tera tera

Who has eaten the chief's dog meat?
We do not know who
May be we do not know where she comes from

The water started covering her feet. Slowly both legs were now into the water. The chief knew she must have been the one. He begged her to tell the truth but she was adamant so she kept trying her luck. Now the whole body was submerged in the water. She was now even failing to sing properly. With time she completely drowned. Wezgera, meaning, "Revenge", her daughter who was present saw how her mother died so she decided to find a way of revenging her mother's death.

One morning she left for the river to a place where her mother drowned. While there she started singing:

Leader:	Cibere camama
All:	Ncamuti yeleyele ncamuti yele
Leader:	Cikule luwiro
All:	Ncamuti yeleyele ncamuti yele

My mother's breast
Grow quickly

So her mother grew into a tall beautiful fruit tree on the river. Then she left for the village and told all the chief's daughters-in-law about nice and tasty fruits at the river. Without further questions they hurried to the river to taste the fruits. When they arrived there, Wezgera told them to climb up the tree and pluck fruits so as to enjoy them better. They happily climbed up the tree. She then started singing the following song:

Leader:	Cibere camama
All:	Ncamuti yeleyele ncamuti yele
Leader:	Ciwenge luwiro
All:	Ncamuti yeleyele ncamuti yele

My mother's breast
Fall down quickly

Suddenly the fruit tree fell down and all the chief's daughters-in-law drowned. Wezgera was happy to have revenged.

Questions
1. What was the chief's hobby?
2. Describe how the chief found out who used to steal meat from his hut.
3. Why did the young girl revenge her mother's death?
4. If you were the chief in this folktale what would you have done in the situation?
5. What lesson/s does this folktale teach on marriage?
6. Create a similar folktale and tell it to your friends.

2
LION AMONG PEOPLE

Once upon a time, there lived a family of two sisters, Ngoza, meaning, "Prick" and, Kasiwa, meaning, "Sleepy" and a brother, Cimutu, meaning, "Big head". Ngoza got married to a lion and the four were happily staying together. As usual, the lion loved hunting so one day he took Cimutu, his brother in law for a hunting escapade in the nearby bush. Upon arrival, they sat down while trying to strategise their hunting.

"I am climbing up the tree and you must cover your face and do not look", said the lion.

Cimutu instantaneously covered his face as the lion climbed up the tree. The lion started singing as follows:

Leader:	Iwe Cimutu
All:	Dingiri nyama na tema dingiri
Leader:	Ungakanena
All:	Dingiri nyama na tema dingiri
Leader:	Kwa mdumbu wako
All:	Dingiri nyama na tema dingiri
Leader:	Ngoza ngwaboza
All:	Dingiri nyama na tema dingiri

You Cimutu,
Do not say anything
To your sister
Ngoza is a liar

Suddenly, quite a few animals came around and the lion killed all of them while Cimutu still covered his face.

"Now you can open your eyes", shouted the lion.

Cimutu was amazed at the slaughter so they returned home with plenty of meat. People at the village were extremely happy. When the meat was over, they went again to hunt. The style was the same with Cimutu covering his face and the lion climbing a tree and singing:

Leader:	Iwe Cimutu
All:	Dingiri nyama na tema dingiri
Leader:	Ungakanena
All:	Dingiri nyama na tema dingiri
Leader:	Kwa mdumbu wako
All:	Dingiri nyama na tema dingiri
Leader:	Ngoza ngwaboza
All:	Dingiri nyama na tema dingiri

You Cimutu,
Do not say anything
To your sister
Ngoza is a liar

Again, they killed a lot of animals and returned home with plenty meat. This time around Ngoza was very suspicious. Something must be happening, she thought, how does he manage to kill all these animals? She asked herself.

"Your friends do not manage to kill this much, how do you manage?" she asked.
"It's all about prowess, my wife", answered the lion smilingly.

One day, on a similar escapade Ngoza decided to follow the lion and Cimutu secretly. When they arrived, the technique was the same with Cimutu covering his face and the lion climbing a tree and singing:

Leader:	Iwe Cimutu
All:	Dingiri nyama na tema dingiri
Leader:	Ungakanena
All:	Dingiri nyama na tema dingiri

Leader:	Kwa mdumbu wako
All:	Dingiri nyama na tema dingiri
Leader:	Ngoza ngwaboza
All:	Dingiri nyama na tema dingiri

You Cimutu,
Do not say anything
To your sister
Ngoza is a liar

Ngoza hid herself within spitting distance. The lion continued singing but no animal came close this time. He wondered and looked at Cimutu but Cimutu's face was still covered as usual. With a loud voice the lion continued to sing but no animal came. Something must have gone wrong somewhere, he thought. Depressed, the lion and Cimutu decided to set out for home. When Ngoza saw that they were about to leave she went ahead of them and started singing the same song while running and dancing in excitement. In the process, unknowingly she dropped her chitenje, a wrap-around cloth, and several beads on the road. As the lion and Cimutu were walking home, they recognised her cloth and beads. The lion now knew why they failed to kill animals. This irritated him.

To add insult to injury, when they reached home, they found the wife pounding and singing the same song:

Leader:	Iwe Cimutu
All:	Dingiri nyama na tema dingiri
Leader:	Ungakanena
All:	Dingiri nyama na tema dingiri
Leader:	Kwa mdumbu wako
All:	Dingiri nyama na tema dingiri
Leader:	Ngoza ngwaboza
All:	Dingiri nyama na tema dingiri

You Cimutu,
Do not say anything
To your sister
Ngoza is a liar

This accelerated the lion's rage so he fumed, jumped and grabbed his wife by the neck and killed her. Meanwhile Cimutu went hiding on top of the house but he unfortunately saw how mercilessly the lion tore up and ate Ngoza. Driven by anger the lion continued the massacre now by eating all villagers who were within his reach. However, after this exhausting activity, he was worn-out and slept. Cimutu then descended to cut open the lion's stomach. Astoundingly, all the people came out alive except Ngoza, the lion's wife.

Questions

1. Explain meanings of the following words as used in the story:
   (a) escapade (b) instantaneous (c) rage (d) massacre
   (e) exhaust (f) astound
2. Explain meanings of the following phrases as used in the story:
   (a) quite a few (b) spitting distance (c) add insult to injury
3. How has the lion been personified in the folktale?
4. What does this folktale tell us about behaviour in marriage?

3
TASTY EGGS

In the olden days in a village, lived several men who used to conduct communal hunting in a close by bush. After the kill, they would amicably share the meat amongst themselves.

One day when they went hunting, they bumped into unusual and wonderful looking eggs.

"Friends they look good, let us try them", one suggested.
"Yes we must taste them", others replied.

They tasted the eggs and found out that they were very tasty. After having enough, they agreed that this should remain a top secret and that no one should carry the eggs to their wives. This was to remain their gift from God.

During the next hunting trip, after a triumphant hunt they went straight to taste tasty eggs and found more than before. While enjoying the wholesome eggs, they reminded one another that it should remain top secret. Indeed, God had showered blessings on them so they could enjoy eggs after hunting.

One of them, however, against the surreptitious agreement, cleverly took two eggs and hid them in the right side pockets of his Bermuda shorts without others noticing him. When he arrived home, he called his wife and his daughter, Muncheya, meaning, "Slim" and gave them the eggs to eat.

"Ooh! How nice they taste, where did you get them from?" said the wife merrily.
"From our hunting escapade, but please do not tell any one that I brought the eggs for you", he replied.
"But I want more, would you please go and get more for me?" she stressed fervently.

Well, the husband seemed persuaded so that one day, before the next communal hunting activity, he decided to go to the bush alone to get the tasty eggs for his wife and his daughter. However, this time he found the owner, a huge snake sitting on its eggs. He was scared and wondered what to do. Suddenly, he remembered a song that he had heard from his grandfather long time ago.

Leader:	Anyina Muncheya mwe
All:	Cidyamudyamu calilima cidyamudyamu
Leader:	Ceneco cafika
All:	Cidyamudyamu calilima cidyamudyamu
Leader:	Ca masumbi ghake
All:	Cidyamudyamu calilima cidyamudyamu
Leader:	Phwaa vicali kunowa
All:	Cidyamudyamu calilima cidyamudyamu

Muncheya's mother
The owner of eggs has come
Phwaa they are still very sweet

The snake slowly slithered away and left the eggs. He served himself and quickly left. The wife was very happy with the eggs and she enjoyed the taste. They developed a happy marriage for the wife felt her husband was a caring man.

"But I want more, would you please go and get more for me?" she asked him again.
"Darling, there is a very big snake, I am afraid it will kill me", he said.
"Ooh! The eggs are very tasty would you please get some more sweetheart?"

Grudgingly but flattered, he set out again for the bush to collect eggs for his sweetheart. When he reached there, he started singing again:

Leader:	Anyina Muncheya mwe
All:	Cidyamudyamu calilima cidyamudyamu
Leader:	Ceneco cafika
All:	Cidyamudyamu calilima cidyamudyamu
Leader:	Ca masumbi ghake
All:	Cidyamudyamu calilima cidyamudyamu
Leader:	Phwaa vicali kunowa
All:	Cidyamudyamu calilima cidyamudyamu

Muncheya's mother
The owner of eggs has come
Phwaa they are still very sweet

The snake was very angry with him. When he finished singing, the snake looked at him and in a flash struck him on the head and killed him. It dragged the corpse and put it together with its eggs. At home the wife waited for a long time for him but he never appeared. Days passed; months passed but the husband was never seen. People at the village were now worried about the whereabouts of their fellow villager and hunter. Where could he have gone? They asked themselves. So they called the wife and asked her about his whereabouts. She explained to them about his last visit to the bush.

"Did he go to the bush alone", they questioned anxiously.

There was no answer from the scared wife who stood speechless, arms akimbo. The village was engulfed with grief. Where could their friend have gone to? What would he have been doing alone in the bush? Would he have broken the secret about eggs? – were questions that lingered in the minds of all the villagers.

The search for a fellow hunter started. All fellow hunters and the lady who enjoyed the eggs went towards the bush. When they arrived there, the hunters advised the wife not to enter into the bush with them. Reaching the place where they used to get eggs, they saw a ferocious snake sitting on the eggs. Fear gripped them but they still sang:

Leader:	Anyina Muncheya mwe
All:	Cidyamudyamu calilima cidyamudyamu
Leader:	Ceneco cafika
All:	Cidyamudyamu calilima cidyamudyamu
Leader:	Ca masumbi ghake
All:	Cidyamudyamu calilima cidyamudyamu
Leader:	Phwaa vicali kunowa
All:	Cidyamudyamu calilima cidyamudyamu

Muncheya's mother
The owner of eggs has come
Phwaa they are still very sweet

The snake then gradually slithered away leaving its eggs and a corpse.

"We told him not to get eggs on his own, what is this now?" they retorted.

Wretchedly, they picked some eggs to take to the woman while some hunters were to come with the corpse later. When they arrived where the woman was, they showed her the eggs first and asked,

"Do you know these?"
"I know them", she said, "My husband used to bring some to me".

The hunters then told her to wait for her husband so as to enjoy the eggs which they had shown her with him. Not knowing what was to come, she felt a little relief. She waited patiently for her husband. But when the men, who were told to carry the corpse arrived, she realised that she had pushed her husband to death and she broke into tears. However, it was too late for her to save him and finally the villagers buried the deceased man.

Questions

1. Make sentences using the following words to show that you understand their meanings:

   (a) triumphant (b) surreptitious (c) Bermuda short (d) fervently (e) slither (f) grudgingly (g) flatter (h) ferocious (i) retort (j) wretch

2. What does this folktale tell us about behaviour in marriage?
3. Describe how the hunters collected eggs from the snake.
4. Visualize and draw how the snake may have looked like.
5. Create a similar folktale and tell it to your friends.

CHAPTER FOUR

Care for Orphans

"Stop crying, the death of your parents should not bother you, we shall take care of you"

INTRODUCTION

Among the Tumbuka people the extended family system is very common and what knits their society is **umoza** *(oneness). This aspect is expressed in different ways. For example, children call their uncles (the brother of your mother or father)* **adada ẁalala** *(elder father) or* **adada ẁacoko** *(younger father) and the same applies to the aunts (the sister of your mother or father) who are called* **amama ẁalala** *or* **amama ẁacoko**. *The use of father or mother even if they are not blood parents brings cohesion amongst the Tumbuka people. In fact, in most cases it is very difficult to know whether the person referred to as father or mother is a real blood parent. This set up made the Tumbuka so closely knit that it was very difficult to notice an orphan amongst them.*

In a typical Tumbuka village children ate together. Food was prepared by every household and given to the children of the village to eat together. It was very difficult to notice an orphan in such a set up. Orphans were not supposed to be isolated from the village since the villages were centres of wisdom where parents spent time telling folktales, riddles, proverbs to the young around the fire place.

With HIV/AIDS rampart in Malaẁi there are a lot of orphans. It would perhaps be beneficial to revisit how our elders cared for orphans. What is paramount is that children raised in a community are given chance to learn values and customs of their society unlike those raised in orphanages that are isolated from their own cultural background. Basically, there is a need to focus on how best the country can keep orphans without making them lose their values and identity.

Many folktales were told to stress the importance of oneness and care among the Tumbuka backed by the popular Tumbuka sayings: **mwana wa munyako ngwako** *(your friend's child or somebody's child is also yours) and* **mwana wamunyako pala wakulira umutole umubape** *(if your friend's child is crying take care of him/her).*

1
A PROSPEROUS MAN

At a certain village long time ago there lived a very prosperous man with his two wives who had a daughter each. The elder wife's daughter was named, Nchaci, meaning, "What for", while the younger wife's Urunji, meaning, "Justice". The two families would cultivate a lot of food enough to feed the whole village during famine.

However, the elderly wife was old and sickly as such it was difficult for her to work at the same rate as the younger wife who was energetic. She, nevertheless, continued to go with the rest of them to work on the farm.

One evening while they were coming from the field singing their favourite traditional song *Nanga unozge caro nchakusuzga* (Even if you can do good things the world/life is full of problems) the elderly wife suddenly collapsed and died. The husband could not believe his eyes, how could his lovely wife go like that? He asked himself.

The younger wife looking nonchalant urged her husband to stop worrying. She did not understand his concern. Her eyes were completely dry. Yes she is gone, now the husband is all for me she thought to herself.

People at the village who had come to the scene assisted in taking care of the situation as the two children were by now weeping uncontrollably. At home the chief was informed and the entombment ceremony took place at the village cemetery. After a few days, all relatives gathered to perform the last ritual, *kumeta*, shaving of hair, to allow them return to their homes and start performing everyday chores.

Life was not the same for the husband. The elder wife who guided him in making serious decisions had gone, indeed gone and gone forever. Besides, the younger wife started behaving strangely as Nchaci was no longer receiving the same care as Urunji.

With problems that were now apparent at home, the husband who was also elderly could not live longer. One day in the late hours he peacefully passed away and was also buried at the village cemetery.

Problems were now apparent for Nchaci. The younger wife asked her to do all household chores while Urunji was busy playing or doing lighter jobs. Nchaci never had a good share of meals any more. When the family was about to eat, she would be sent to draw water from the river several kilometers away from the village. For sure, she missed meal times and fed only on leftovers. Nobody really cared for her.

After pondering on her situation Nchaci decided to seek help from her late mother. How could she do this? She kept pondering. Well, one day she decided to go to the village cemetery and sit on her mother's tombstone while singing the following song:

Leader:	Amama Ukani
All:	Songa Mbiriŵiri
Leader:	Amama Ukani
All:	Songa Mbiriŵiri
	Leka nakuwona wa mwana wane
	Songa mbiriŵiri
	Kwaca civwelekete cinthu ici naco
	Songa mbiriŵiri

Mother rise from the dead
Mother rise from the dead
I have seen you my daughter
Let me rise

After singing sombrely for a long time her mother rose from the dead. Her child looked miserable so she bathed, fed and clad her in new clothes before suddenly disappearing into her grave. Nchaci happily descended to the village from the village cemetery that overlooked the village.

When she arrived home, the younger wife was surprised to see her energetic and in new clothes. Would she have found a suitor? She asked herself inwardly. The next day, Nchaci also left to seek help from her mother at the village cemetery and sang again solemnly:

Leader:	Amama Ukani
All:	Songa Mbiriŵiri
Leader:	Amama Ukani
All:	Songa Mbiriŵiri
	Leka nakuwona wa mwana wane
	Songa mbiriŵiri
	Kwaca civwelekete cinthu ici naco
	Songa mbiriŵiri

Mother rise from the dead
Mother rise from the dead
I have seen you my daughter
Let me rise

Her mother appeared again and also bathed, fed and clad her in new clothes before suddenly disappearing into her grave. Well, Nchaci did this for a few more days while the younger wife was seriously asking herself inwardly what was happening to the young girl.

One day as Nchaci went to the village cemetery again, the younger wife decided to follow her. What could she be doing here? She asked herself. The girl went straight to her mother's tombstone, sat and started singing solemnly:

Leader:	Amama Ukani
All:	Songa Mbiriŵiri
Leader:	Amama Ukani
All:	Songa Mbiriŵiri
	Leka nakuwona wa mwana wane
	Songa mbiriŵiri
	Kwaca civwelekete cinthu ici naco
	Songa mbiriŵiri

Mother rise from the dead
Mother rise from the dead
I have seen you my daughter
Let me rise

As usual her late mother rose from the dead, bathed, fed and clad her in new clothes before disappearing into her grave. Immediately, the younger wife started howling.

"Nchaci forgive me if I have led you to this", she said with a throaty frail tone, "forgive, forgiiiive, forgiiiiive meee …" and she too collapsed and died.

Questions

1. Explain meanings of the following words as used in the story:
   (a) prosperous (b) collapse (c) nonchalant (d) entombment (e) cemetery (f) ritual (g) ponder (h) sombre (i) clad.
2. Who are the characters in the above folktale?
3. Explain how Nchaci suffered? Does this happen today? Share your experiences.
4. What does this folktale teach about orphans?
5. Create a similar folktale and tell it to your friends.

2
A HUSBAND WITH TWO WIVES

Long ago, a man married two wives. The women mothered a daughter each. Temwaci, meaning, "Love", was the daughter of the elder wife and, Cidongo, meaning, "From the Soil" was the daughter of the young wife. The man loved his daughters so that every time he went away he returned with gifts ranging from sweets to clothes for them. With time, the younger wife who was unhealthy passed away so the elder wife was keeping the two daughters. She did not like Cidongo at all such that she devised a plot to kill her.

One day she called the two girls and told them to draw water from the village *mthombo*, well, a few kilometres away from the house. She gave to her daughter a leaky pail and to Cidongo a good one. For sure it was difficult for Temwaci to draw water properly. Well Cidongo with a perfect pail quickly drew water and set out for home. Upon arrival, she was greeted by an angry elder mother who stood conspicuously waiting for her.

> "I was looking for you, stupid girl", she angrily said, "You make my daughter suffer here as if you belong to this family."

She quickly grabbed her by the neck while the water spilt, threw her in a hole and buried her completely. The child cried out for help but no one was near to hear her cry.

Failing to draw water properly, Temwaci also walked home.

> "You gave me a leaky pail, mum, I have failed to draw water, but where is Cidongo? She asked.
> "Do not ask me where that stupid girl is, I thought you were together at the well, was I there?" answered the mother.

The girl quickly shut up. But she kept wondering what could have happened. The mood at home was very sombre. After a few days, Cidongo while buried in the earth started singing:

Leader:	Temwaci Temwaci
All:	Temwaci Temwaci
Leader:	Adada ŵafika Temwaci
All:	Temwaci Temwaci
All:	Ŵayeya viwemi Temwaci

Temwaci
Temwaci
Our father has come, Temwaci
He has carried good things, Temwaci

Upon hearing the song Cidongo called her mother to come and listen to the strange but interesting song coming from behind the house. The mother was not happy with the news so she warned her never to listen to the song again.

The next day Cidongo, started singing again:

Leader:	Temwaci Temwaci
All:	Temwaci Temwaci
Leader:	Namunyako wanijimira kalinde Temwaci

All:	Temwaci Temwaci
Leader:	Sisi lane la chesama
All:	Temwaci

Temwaci Temwaci
Temwaci Temwaci
I have been buried in the earth, Temwaci
My hair has now become red Temwaci

The girl listened attentively and recognised the voice of Cidongo so she started responding to the song.

Leader:	Temwaci Temwaci
All:	Temwaci Temwaci
Leader:	Namunyako wanijimira kalinde Temwaci

All:	Temwaci Temwaci
Leader:	Sisi lane la chesama
All:	Temwaci

Temwaci Temwaci
Temwaci Temwaci
I have been buried in the earth, Temwaci
My hair has now become red Temwaci

The singing became louder and louder as the villagers came to see what was happening. Now the message was clear: something must have happened to Cidongo. Villagers glared at Temwaci's mother who kept sweating profusely.

When the father arrived, he was very surprised at what was taking place.

"What is happening behind my house?" asked the father apprehensively.
"Father, come and listen, Cidongo is singing here", answered Temwaci.
"Strange, strange, we need explanation!" shouted the villagers.

They went closer to the spot and the girl buried in the earth started singing again:

Leader:	Temwaci Temwaci
All:	Temwaci Temwaci
Leader:	Namunyako wanijimira kalinde Temwaci
All:	Temwaci Temwaci
Leader:	Sisi lane la chesama
All:	Temwaci

Temwaci Temwaci
Temwaci Temwaci
I have been buried in the earth, Temwaci
My hair has now become red Temwaci

The father in deep sorrow called his wife to explain the strange happening that had now become the talk of the village. The woman was very frightened and was sweating profusely. She could hardly move her lips to speak. She had tried to kill Cidongo. While the villagers assisted in excavating the child from the earth, the wife was taken to the village court for further questioning.

Questions

1. Explain meanings of the following words as used in the story:
   (a) profusely (b) conspicuously (c) apprehensively (d) excavate
2. Who are the characters in the above folktale?
3. What problems of orphans does this folktale reveal?
4. Discuss the merits and demerits of polygamy.
5. Create a similar folktale and tell it to your friends.

3
CHILDREN

In the olden days, there lived an old woman with two daughters. The elder, Masuzgo, meaning, "Trouble" and the younger, Masozi, meaning, "Tears". Since the old woman was ailing she advised her daughters to take care of each other when she died. Since Masuzgo was the elder and ready for marriage, it was expected that she would keep her sister as the extended family demanded.

Indeed, after some time Masuzgo wedded and followed her husband to a remote place. So Masozi stayed alone with her mother. Unfortunately, it was not long after Masuzgo's marriage that the mother passed away and was buried.

Masozi, then one day, set out to stay with her sister in a remote place. When she arrived there she was told that her job was to chase birds that were destroying rice on the farm. It was to become her life forever. Indeed early in the morning she would go to the rice farm to chase birds for the whole day only to return late in the night. She was not given food or soap for her bath and eventually she became very miserable. While chasing birds she expressed her misery in the following song:

Leader:	Fya Mbalame
All:	Kajenjelekete kajenjelekete yaa
Leader:	Amama wakanituma
All:	Kajenjelekete kajenjelekete yaa
Leader:	Ine pala nafwa
All:	Kajenjelekete kajenjelekete yaa
	Ulute kwa mkulu wako
	Mkulu wane wanizgora muzga

Birds go away
My mother sent me
That when she dies
I should live with my sister
My sister has made me a slave

The birds while enjoying the rice used to listen to her moving song. With time they became very concerned with her plight so they decided to start preparing food for her. She would eat and go to sleep at home. After some time, the elder sister was surprised to see that she was very brawny even after spending several days without food.

This happened for several times; so one day as Masozi went to the rice farm Masuzgo decided to follow her so she could see what was making her sister brawny. As soon as Masozi arrived at the farm she started singing her moving song:

Leader:	Fya Mbalame
All:	Kajenjelekete kajenjelekete yaa
Leader:	Amama wakanituma
All:	Kajenjelekete kajenjelekete yaa
Leader:	Ine pala nafwa
All:	Kajenjelekete kajenjelekete yaa
	Ulute kwa mkulu wako
	Mkulu wane wanizgora muzga

Birds go away
My mother sent me
That when she dies
I should live with my sister
My sister has made me a slave

As usual, the birds prepared nice food for her. Masuzgo saw everything and was very sad for she knew that she had made her sister a slave. She cried sorrowfully and took her sister home.

Questions

1. Explain meanings of the following words as used in the story:
   (a) ail (b) wed (c) remote (d) appropriate (e) plight (f) brawny
2. Who are the characters in the above folktale?
3. What piece of advice did the mother give to the daughters?
4. What type of work was given to the younger daughter when she stayed with her elder sister?
5. What lesson on orphans does this folktale teach us?
6. Create a similar folktale and tell it to your friends.

Many folktales were told to express the importance of oneness and care among the Tumbuka backed by popular Tumbuka sayings: *mwana wamunyako ngwako (Your friend's child or somebody's child is yours) and mwana wamunyako pala wakulira umutole umubape (if your friend's child is crying, take care of him/her)*

CHAPTER FIVE

Good Behaviour

"Let me help you mama"

INTRODUCTION

Among the Tumbuka people, good conduct is paramount. Good behaviour or accepted behaviour is a sign of proper upbringing. If one conducts himself well, it is believed that he will keep his relatives well and maintain the extended family properly. Good behaviour can be expressed in different ways and experiences. It is the behaviour that one must have whether in marriage, among the peers, at school and in several other circumstances.

Today, society seriously lacks well-behaved people. Most children lack proper upbringing as regards behaviour. In Malaŵi, just like in many other countries, this has affected school discipline seriously as students have become very unruly. Since children are future leaders their bad behaviour reflects negatively on the leadership of their countries and societies. It is not too late to turn to what our parents taught on behaviour and learn from them.

1
FATHER AND SON

Long time ago in a village lived a father, Masuzgo, meaning, "Troubles" and his son Kawezgera, meaning, "Revenge". The father kept a very big snake in a clay pot, which was covered tightly. He advised his son never to touch and open the clay pot.

One day, after quite a few weeks, Kawezgera decided to see what was in the clay pot so he started singing:

Leader:	Cinthu ca ŵadada
All:	Jinjiwe jinji yaya jinjiwe jinji
Leader:	Sono mufumenge
All:	Jinjiwe jinji yaya jinjiwe jinji

The property of my father
Now come out

The snake slowly started unfurling itself until it came out of the pot. Terrified, he wanted to run away but stood firm. Surprisingly, the big snake started dancing to the song. Indeed, the more he sang the more the snake danced. After some time he wanted the snake to go back into the pot so he sang again:

Leader:	Cinthu ca ŵadada
All:	Jinjiwe jinji yaya jinjiwe jinji
Leader:	Sono munjirenge
Leader:	Ŵeneko wakwiza
All:	Jinjiwe jinji yaya jinjiwe jinji

The property of my father
Now go back into the pot
The owner is coming

The snake then went back into the pot.

He thought this was very exciting so the next day when the father was also away, he decided to call his friends to watch the snake dance. When his friends arrived he started singing:

Leader:	Cinthu ca ŵadada
All:	Jinjiwe jinji yaya jinjiwe jinji
Leader:	Sono mufumenge
All:	Jinjiwe jinji yaya jinjiwe jinji

The property of my father
Now come out

All his friends were surprised at the way the snake danced. It was strange and amazing. When it was a bit late, fearing that his father would find him, he decided to make the snake go back into the pot, so he sang:

Leader:	Cinthu ca ŵadada
All:	Jinjiwe jinji yaya jinjiwe jinji
Leader:	Sono munjirenge
All:	Jinjiwe jinji yaya jinjiwe jinji
Leader:	Ŵeneko ŵakwiza
All:	Jinjiwe jinji yaya jinjiwe jinji

The property of my father
Now go back into the pot
The owner is coming

The snake slowly entered into the pot which he tightly covered.

News of the dancing snake spread like bush fire. Villagers were alerted that whenever his father was away, Kawezgera started the show. The other day when his father was away again, Kawezgera called his friends again and started singing:

Leader:	Cinthu ca ŵadada
All:	Jinjiwe jinji yaya jinjiwe jinji
Leader:	Sono mufumenge
All:	Jinjiwe jinji yaya jinjiwe jinji

The property of my father
Now come out

The snake came out and danced. Everybody was happy. When it was getting late, he decided to take it back into the pot, so he sang:

Leader:	Cinthu ca ŵadada
All:	Jinjiwe jinji yaya jinjiwe jinji
Leader:	Sono munjirenge
All:	Jinjiwe jinji yaya jinjiwe jinji
Leader:	Ŵeneko ŵakwiza
All:	Jinjiwe jinji yaya jinjiwe jinji

The property of my father
Now go back into the pot
The owner is coming

This time he sang for a long time but the snake did not respond as usual. Suddenly, with anger it lifted its head, stretched itself and ran towards the river at great speed while everybody ran for his or her life. There was pandemonium.

When the father arrived, he went straight to check his snake in the pot.

"Where is my snake, Kawezgera?" he asked.

Kawezgera hesitated for some time but finally in a choking voice, answered,

"I...I...I was playing with it so it has escaped to the river."
"What! You mean it has run away, please go and look for it", said the father furiously.

The two then went to look for the lost snake. Kawezgera went into the river and started catching things, which he kept showing his father for identification. While undertaking this task, he sang the following song:

Leader: Ni ici adada, ni ici adada
All: Nchilungulungu maji taya, taya taya
            Nchilungulungu maji taya.

Is it this one father, is it this one
It's a useless water animal throw it away,
Throw it away.

He searched for a long time but did not find the snake. His father was so angry that he vowed to disown his son if the snake would not be found next time.   They, however, left for home together.

The next day, as usual, the father went away. Kawezgera decided to collect a grasshopper which he put in the cup that his father used for drinking water. When the father came back, feeling thirsty, he went straight and picked up the cup in order to drink some water. The moment he lifted the cup, the grasshopper flew away and away it went.

"Where is my grasshopper, father?" asked Kawezgera.

"You know I wanted to drink water, but the grasshopper flew away and I failed to get it", the father answered.

"Father, go and look for it now!" commanded the son.

The father then started off to look for his son's grasshopper while singing:

Leader:	Phananana wa mwana wane
All:	Dekanitole phanana, dekanitole
Leader:	Phululu soce
All:	Dekanitole phanana, dekanitole

My son's grasshopper
Come down, I want to pick you
Flying up and down
Come down, I want to pick you

The father spent several days looking for the grasshopper but could not find it.

Questions

1. What lessons can you draw from this folktale?
2. Explain the importance of good conduct in modern society.
3. Describe how Kawezgera made the snake dance.
4. In groups create songs in your language similar to the ones in the folktale

2
THE BIRD OF TRUTH

Once upon a time, there was a very big village in Nyasaland. Elders, sons, daughters, daughters-in-law inhabited the village. Since life was difficult in the village three men from the village (Komani, Nyifwa and Malikande) left their wives for the mines in Johannesburg. They worked there for a long time.

While in Johannesburg, Komani and Nyifwa mostly spent their salaries on beer and other interesting things in the new land. It was said that in the township where they stayed they were the most popular foreigners. However, Malikande spent his money carefully and saved enough for his relatives at home. He knew that he had more responsibility at home in Nyasaland than in Johannesburg. After working for a year, the three men had a holiday and so decided to go home to Nyasaland to see their parents, wives and relatives.

From Johannesburg to Nyasaland was a long way so people used to walk for several days and months before they reached their homes. It was said that they passed through Harare where they also saw tall buildings like those in Johannesburg. However, mostly they walked through the bush where they would sleep for days and start their journey again.

When they were a few kilometres from home, Komani and Nyifwa realised that they did not have much luggage to share among relatives at home. As the three men got closer to their home there was sudden change in their conversation. While Malikande was happy to reach home the other two kept silent remembering the way they held the big beer bottles in beer halls.

Malikande was busy carrying his luggage full of gifts for his parents, wife and children. However, Komani and Nyifwa fearing disappointing their parents and relatives decided to kill Malikande. After killing him, they shared the loot between themselves. They were now very happy because they could show their parents that they had been working very hard.

As they walked for some kilometres away, they found a bird that started singing:

Leader:	Yelele Malikande, yelele Malikande
All:	Yelele Malikande
Leader:	Vinyamata
All:	Yelele Malikande
Leader:	Vya pa Joni
All:	Yelele Malikande
Leader:	Vyagwazana
All:	Yelele Malikande
Leader:	Vyatolako
All:	Yelele Malikande
Leader:	Cuma cake
All:	Yelele Malikande
Leader:	Vyagawana
All:	Yelele Malikande
Leader:	Wakuteta wakuteta nawawona
All:	Yelele Malikande

Men from Johannesburg
Have stabbed their friend
They have shared his wealth
They should not cheat, I have seen them

The two started asking each other about what the bird was singing. Could it be that someone saw them, they thought aloud. They listened to the bird again and it sang the same piercing song. They brushed it aside and continued to walk home. After a short walk, the bird started to sing again. Now they caught the bird, killed it and threw it into the bush. They waited for some time, but the bird sang no more. Happily they started off again. They shared stories and jokes they learnt while drinking in Johannesburg and wondered why countries were so different. They shared their fears and went on. Suddenly, they found the bird in front of them again singing the same piercing song:

Leader:	Yelele Malikande, yelele Malikande
All:	Yelele Malikande
Leader:	Vinyamata
All:	Yelele Malikande
Leader:	Vya pa Joni
All:	Yelele Malikande
Leader:	Vyagwazana
All:	Yelele Malikande
Leader:	Vyatolako
All:	Yelele Malikande
Leader:	Cuma cake
All:	Yelele Malikande
Leader:	Vyagawana
All:	Yelele Malikande
Leader:	Wakuteta wakuteta nawawona
All:	Yelele Malikande

Men from Johannesburg
Have stabbed their friend
They have shared his wealth
They should not cheat, I have seen them

Surprised, they caught the bird yet again and this time around took some firewood, made a fire and burnt it to ashes. They were now very sure that the bird could not appear again as they continued their journey to the village and shared stories about their wealth and so on. This time around, the bird did not sing until when they reached close to their home. The bird went on top of a very tall tree and started singing again:

Leader:	Yelele Malikande, yelele Malikande
All:	Yelele Malikande
Leader:	Vinyamata
All:	Yelele Malikande
Leader:	Vya pa Joni
All:	Yelele Malikande

Leader:	Vyagwazana
All:	Yelele Malikande
Leader:	Vyatolako
All:	Yelele Malikande
Leader:	Cuma cake
All:	Yelele Malikande
Leader:	Vyagawana
All:	Yelele Malikande
Leader:	Wakuteta wakuteta nawawona
All:	Yelele Malikande

Men from Johannesburg
Have stabbed their friend
They have shared his wealth
They should not cheat, I have seen them

Now they became very anxious so they ignored the bird and its provocative song until they reached home. People were very happy to see them back from work. Their wives danced for they knew their husbands had come with wealth.

"Where is Malikande your friend?" asked one elderly person.
"He is very happy in Johannesburg so he will come next year, besides, he got a better job than us", they answered.
"He, for sure, is the cleverest of the three, I am not surprised to hear this", said Malikande's father.

They laughed and continued with other stories about cars, and tall buildings in Johannesburg and so on. Women brought food but just before the village feast started, the bird went on top of the hut and started singing again:

Leader:	Yelele Malikande, yelele Malikande
All:	Yelele Malikande
Leader:	Vinyamata
All:	Yelele Malikande
Leader:	Vya pa Joni
All:	Yelele Malikande

Leader:	Vyagwazana
All:	Yelele Malikande
Leader:	Vyatolako
All:	Yelele Malikande
Leader:	Cuma cake
All:	Yelele Malikande
Leader:	Vyagawana
All:	Yelele Malikande
Leader:	Wakuteta wakuteta nawawona
All:	Yelele Malikande

Men from Johannesburg
Have stabbed their friend
They have shared his wealth
They should not cheat, I have seen them

People were surprised. They went out and listened to the song.

"The bird is saying that these two have killed Malikande and have taken his wealth", said one good listener among the villagers.

Members of the village flocked to the house and listened to the bird singing. It was later revealed that the bird was telling the truth.

Questions

1. Describe the setting of the story.
2. What does this story tell us about behaviour?
3. Explain how the bird revealed what happened to Malikande.
4. How does laziness affect your society today?
5. Do you know any other story which depicts similar events?

3
LION AND HYENA
___

One upon a time, lion and hyena were friends. They befriended each other for along time and used to play and hunt together. They even shared stories about their girlfriends.

One day hyena asked lion to escort him to the home of his prospective mate.

> "That is beautiful", said the lion, "When should that be?" he continued.
> "As soon as possible, I am tired of staying alone, I need a wife", said hyena.

So the next day they started off to see hyena's prospective spouse.

> "I am happy that we are going to see your prospective wife because what we want is that you should have a wife. But knowing you, if something bad happens you will have yourself to blame", warned the lion.

The hyena kept silent.

As they walked for some kilometres, hyena smelt something meaty smell from the bush.

> "Excuse me friend, I would like to urinate in the bush, I will find you", he said.

While the lion walked slowly waiting for him, hyena branched into the bush and started looking for the meat. He found succulent meat so he quickly enjoyed the feast. He then happily followed the lion who had become a little suspicious of him.

Well the journey continued and they shared stories about beautiful girls they had ever known. They walked again for a long time for the place was exceedingly far. Passing near a village, hyena branched yet again.

"Excuse me friend, I would like to urinate in the bush, I will find you", he said.

The lion kept silent and walked slowly waiting for his friend. This time the hyena saw chickens wandering near the neighbourhood. He caught some and fed himself. He then happily followed the lion that had become suspicious of his urinating habits.

Well, the journey continued and they continued to share stories about beautiful girls in their vicinity. A few kilometres before they arrived, they saw goats feeding near the bush. Hyena salivating said to lion:

"Excuse me friend, I would like to urinate in the bush, I will find you", he said.

The lion kept silent and walked slowly waiting for his urinating friend. This time the hyena chased the goats, caught some and enjoyed the meat. He then happily followed the lion that had now become irritated.

They were now approaching their destination. Soon they arrived and the parents of the girl happily welcomed them and brought them into the house. The villagers prepared nice food for lion and hyena that they ate and no one would be expected to feel hungry again that night. They were undeniably very pleased. As was the custom the parents later brought in the girl and asked her if she was interested to marry Hyena and she accepted. The mood in the house was good-humoured and everyone was dancing.

By night fall the event was through so everybody went to rest and sleep. While lion was sleeping the hyena woke up, opened the door and went to the village kraal and started slaughtering innocent goats and eating the meat. A great bleating noise of dying goats was heard so the villagers woke up.

"Thieves, thieves, our goats are dying!" shouted the one whose house was closer to the kraal.

All the villagers woke up and found the hyena feeding on goats. The lion woke up and was very disappointed with his friend. He was left dumbstricken. The villagers chased them away. Regretfully and expectedly hyena failed to tie the knot with the girl.

Questions

1. Explain how hyena and lion have been personified in this folktale?
2. Explain how the hyena failed to marry?
3. How do people in your village conduct themselves when they want to marry?
4. What do the following expressions mean?
   Good-humoured (b) tie the knot (c) dumbstricken
5. Describe any five qualities of a husband or a wife you would like to marry.
6. With reference to modern life, explain lessons this folktale teaches on behaviour.

CHAPTER SIX

Warning Against Beasts

"Aaa a lion, I must run for my life"

INTRODUCTION

Every society has its fears. Naturally, society finds ways to bring awareness among its people against its fears or enemies. Among the Tumbuka society the common enemies in the old days were beasts or wild animals. The elders used some folktales to warn the youth and society at large against numerous beasts that existed in their vicinity. The most common beasts were hyenas, leopards, lions, snakes and elephants.

Modern Malaŵi society undoubtedly has its own enemies different from these. How can society bring awareness among the people about modern dangers? The tales following show how the elders among the Tumbuka people warned society against beasts.

1
FOUR GIRLS AND A GRANDMOTHER

Four girls once lived with their grandmother in a village. The grandmother kept telling the four that what mattered in life was proper education so that they could uplift themselves economically. She spent most of her time teaching them about good behaviour. However, the girls used to spend time with their boyfriends at night and used to cheat their grandmother that they were going to school to study. Since the place was inhabited with dangerous wild animals, every time they came back from their endeavours they sang the following song while mentioning their names for the grandmother to recognise them:

Leader:	Gogo julire
All:	Kayiya tate julire kayiya
Leader:	Ndine Goli
All	Kayiya tate julire kayiya
Leader:	Nafuma kusukulu
All:	Kayiya tate julire kayiya
Leader:	Ndine Nyuma
All:	Kayiya tate julire kayiya
Leader:	Nafuma kusukulu

All:	Kayiya tate julire kayiya
Leader:	Ndine Zgangose
All:	Kayiya tate julire kayiya
Leader:	Nafuma kusukulu
All:	Kayiya tate julire kayiya
Leader:	Ndine Ilinase
All:	Kayiya tate julire kayiya
Leader:	Nafuma kusukulu
All:	Kayiya tate julire kayiya

Grandmother open for us
I am Goli, please open
I have come from school
I am Nyuma, please open
I have come from school
I am Zgangose, please open
I have come from school
I am Ilinase, please open
I have come from school

The grandmother would open for them and shout at them for coming late.

"You cannot tell me that you are coming from school at this time, I do not want this to happen again," she would retort.

The girls would keep quiet and sleep innocently. The next night, they would slip away again to visit their boy friends and come back late singing the same song for the grandmother to open for them:

Leader:	Gogo julire
All:	Kayiya tate julire kayiya
Leader:	Ndine Goli
All	Kayiya tate julire kayiya
Leader:	Nafuma kusukulu
All:	Kayiya tate julire kayiya
Leader:	Ndine Nyuma
All:	Kayiya tate julire kayiya
Leader:	Nafuma kusukulu

All:	Kayiya tate julire kayiya
Leader:	Ndine Zgangose
All:	Kayiya tate julire kayiya
Leader:	Nafuma kusukulu
All:	Kayiya tate julire kayiya
Leader:	Ndine Ilinase
All:	Kayiya tate julire kayiya
Leader:	Nafuma kusukulu
All:	Kayiya tate julire kayiya

Grandmother open for us
I am Goli, please open
I have come from school
I am Nyuma, please open
I have come from school
I am Zgangose, please open
I have come from school
I am Ilinase, please open
I have come from school

The grandmother would open for them painfully and warn them as usual.

One day, a hyena that was listening to the song came and sang for the grandmother to open. However, the grandmother recognised the strangeness of the voice and so did not open. When the girls came, she told them that there was an animal that was singing the same song and that the girls were putting her in great danger. The girls brushed this off and continued with their mischief.

The hyena having failed to sing properly, now decided to wait for the girls and capture them. One night, the girls came and started singing:

Leader:	Gogo julire
All:	Kayiya tate julire kayiya
Leader:	Ndine Goli
All	Kayiya tate julire kayiya
Leader:	Nafuma Kusukulu

All:	Kayiya tate julire kayiya
Leader:	Ndine Nyuma
All:	Kayiya tate julire kayiya
Leader:	Nafuma kusukulu
All:	Kayiya tate julire kayiya
Leader:	Ndine Zgangose
All:	Kayiya tate julire kayiya
Leader:	Nafuma kusukulu
All:	Kayiya tate julire kayiya
Leader:	Ndine Ilinase
All:	Kayiya tate julire kayiya
Leader:	Nafuma kusukulu
All:	Kayiya tate julire kayiya

Grandmother open for us
I am Goli, please open
I have come from school
I am Nyuma, please open
I have come from school
I am Zgangose, please open
I have come from school
I am Ilinase, please open
I have come from school

After singing for a long time, the grandmother was tired and did not open for them. The hyena that was hiding nearby slowly stalked and captured Goli, the elder daughter. The three started crying while singing for their grandmother to open the door. When the grandmother heard the cry she opened, only to be told that a hyena had captured Goli.

Questions

1. How does the folktale stress the importance of advice from the elderly?
2. Describe how Goli may have been captured.
3. What lessons can we draw from the folktale today?
4. Why did the girls slip away at night?

2
HYENA AND KALULU THE HARE

Hyena and Kalulu the hare were good friends once upon a time. Kalulu the hare was employed while hyena was not so every time Kalulu the hare left for work, he told his wife to be careful with people who came to visit her. Indeed, every time he arrived home, he sang a special song for the wife to recognise his voice.

Leader:	Jeni Jeni nijulileko
All:	Kamtetekakamteteka kaa
Leader:	Mwaluwaci?
All:	Naluwa nthonga kamtetekakamteteka kaa

Jane, Jane open for me
What have you forgotten?
I have forgotten a club

Hyena being a dangerous and greedy animal always planned to kill his friend's wife. He tried several ways to catch her. He went and knocked at her door several times but was not allowed in. One day he decided to hide near the home to discover how his friend entered the house. After work and innocently, Kalulu the hare came and sang his usual song for the wife to open the door for him.

Leader:	Jeni Jeni nijulileko
All:	Kamtetekakamteteka kaa
Leader:	Mwaluwaci?
All:	Naluwa nthonga kamtetekakamteteka kaa

Jane, Jane open for me
What have you forgotten?
I have forgotten a club

Hyena listened carefully. The next day, just before his friend came, he went to his friend's house and started singing the same song. However, the singing was so awful that the wife of Kalulu the hare noticed it was not her husband. She, therefore, did not open. After a few minutes, Kalulu the hare arrived and sang his song properly.

Leader:	Jeni Jeni nijulileko
All:	Kamtetekakamteteka kaa
Leader:	Mwaluwaci?
All:	Naluwa nthonga kamtetekakamteteka kaa

Jane open for me
What have you forgotten?
I have forgotten a club

His wife opened and said, "Did you change your voice a few minutes ago?"

"No why could I do that my dear wife?" answered the husband.
"Then there was someone else who tried to sing your song" she insisted.
"No, you must have been dreaming", Kalulu the hare dismissed his wife's claim.

The next few days hyena still hid near the house to get the right tune. One day he went again to the house and sang exactly like Kalulu the hare. When the wife opened, he killed her and dragged her away to the bush to enjoy the fresh meat. When Kalulu the hare arrived, he was surprised to see the house was empty and marks of fresh blood around the house. Could it be that my wife has been killed, he thought. He called people around the village and asked them to assist him look for his dear wife. They, unfortunately, found out that Hyena had killed her.

It was too late for him. The truth was that he was going to live without his dear wife forever.

Questions
1. Describe how Hyena killed Kalulu the hare's wife.
2. Describe the setting in this folktale.
3. How does this folktale warn society about dangerous animals?
4. What is the significance of personification in this folktale?
5. What enemies interfere with your society today and how is your society forewarned?

"How can society bring awareness among the people about modern dangers?"

CHAPTER SEVEN

Respect for Elders

"Well my son, remember to respect your teachers at school"

INTRODUCTION

Among the Tumbuka, elderly people or parents are regarded as the most experienced and indeed guardians of wisdom. They define behaviour for the youth. In some circles, the elders have been called **ẁaciuta wa pano pasi** *(gods on earth) to stress their significance in assisting and moulding society. There is a strong belief among the Tumbuka that if parents are not happy with a child, the child does not find luck in whatever he or she does. This respect, however, does not translate into blind reverence.*

Today, most young people rebel against their parents due to several reasons. Undoubtedly, society needs to reflect on how to teach the youth to respect the elderly people or parents whether they are at home, at school or indeed at work. The Tumbuka taught respect through folktales such as these below:

1
THE YOUTHFUL RULE

Once upon a time, in a very big village, lived many people. As usual elders ruled the village. However, the youth in the village did not like the way the elders ruled.

One day, all the youth of the village gathered and decided to get rid of all the old people of the village in order to end the conservative type of rule. A big battle followed that wiped the elderly and the youth were very happy to establish their youthful rule. However, there was one boy who hid his father in the mountains and every morning he secretly went to feed him.

One night while the youthful chief was sleeping, a fearful snake constricted him. As a result he could not breathe properly. His wife was afraid that the chief was going to die. She did not know what to do. She called the villagers to assist.

The youth ran to the house to rescue their endangered chief. Upon reaching the house, they saw their chief constricted by a fierce snake that kept its head dangling in the air looking for anybody who tried to come any closer. Meanwhile, the chief was gasping for air. The mood was characterised by wailing women and was solemn. The youth who did not know what to do were now watching their chief die slowly and painfully.

As the situation kept worsening, the boy who had hid his father in the mountains shouted,

"I know of someone who can help us rescue our chief"
"Go and get the person here immediately," chorused the youth.
"I will go unless you promise that nothing bad will happen to the person," said the boy anxiously.
"Go and get the person here immediately," chorused the youth.

The boy then rushed to the mountain and told his father the problem at hand. They rushed together to the chief's house.

"Why has he brought his father?" murmured some of the youth.
"Stop the nonsense, let him rescue our chief!" shouted the more concerned ones.

The old man demanded that a few people stay away from the room for air to circulate properly. He then asked a few boys to rush to the river and fetch a frog. This they did very quickly. He then tied the frog to a long string and told one boy to show and put it close to the snake that constricted the chief. The chief's eyes were bulging. However, upon seeing the frog, the snake started to slowly move towards the frog. The old man commanded the boy to keep pulling the string gradually further and further away so that the snake should follow to catch the frog. Indeed the snake followed and by so doing relieving the chief of his pain. The chief started breathing better. Indeed, the boy kept pulling the string slowly until the snake left the chief completely as it followed the frog and they killed it.

The youth thanked the boy who hid his father. They now realised the importance of elderly people in their society.

Questions

1. Who are the characters in this folktale?
2. Describe the setting of this folktale.
3. What does this folktale tell us about elderly people among the Tumbuka?
4. Imagine the scene and draw the chief constricted by a snake.
5. In your own words narrate this folktale to others.
6. Discuss whether it is important to respect elders in your society

2
MOTHER, DAUGHTER AND GROUNDNUT FIELD

Once upon a time, there lived a mother with a daughter, Soka, meaning, "Bad Luck", whom she loved dearly. She was a hardworking farmer with a very big groundnut field and she used to send Soka to collect firewood from the bush.

The mother advised Soka that she was allowed to dig only one groundnut a day from the field, whenever she came back from the bush. The instruction was to be adhered to strictly. For a long time, Soka followed the instructions very well.

One day, tired and hungry from the bush, she dug only one and left for home. While at home and since she was not full she decided to return to the field to dig the second one. This one she ate very quickly for she was afraid of her mother. She then hastily decided to leave the field but unfortunately she could not manage to move out. She stood motionless and wondered. Suddenly, she noticed that her legs started sinking into the earth. Worried, she decided to sing:

Leader:	Amama
All:	Zanikuno
Leader:	Amama
All:	Zanikuno
Leader:	Amama mukayowoya, amama imwe
All:	Zanikuno
Leader:	Nijime yimo yimo, amama imwe
All:	Zanikuno
Leader:	Najima ziwiri nananga, amama imwe
All:	Zanikuno
Leader:	Sono nkhunjira pasi, amama imwe
All:	Zanikuno

Mum
Come here
Mum you said
Come here
I should only dig one
Come here
I have dug two I have wronged you
Come here
Now I am getting buried into the earth
Come here

Then the mother heard the voice of her daughter, she rushed to the scene but alas could not do anything. Her child had failed to follow the rule.

"I told you to dig only one why did you dig two?" cried the mother.

The daughter kept singing as she slowly sunk into the earth, now with a choking voice she sang:

Leader:	Aaamama
All:	Zaanikuno
Leader:	Aaamama
All:	Zaanikuno
Leader:	Aamama muukaayowoya, aaamama imwe
All:	Zaanikuno
Leader:	Niijime yimo yimo, aaamama imwe
All:	Zaanikuno
Leader:	Najiiima ziiiwiri nananga, aaamama imwe
All:	Zaaanikuno
Leader:	Soono nkhunjira pasi, aaamama imwe
All:	Zaaanikuno

Mum
Come here
Mum you said
Come here
I should only dig one
Come here
I have dug two I have wronged you
Come here
Now I am getting buried into the earth
Come here

The mother also stood outside the garden as villagers looked on in sorrow. Gradually, the voice faded as Soka got buried in the soil completely.

Questions

1. Describe Soka's death.
2. Explain lessons we can draw from this folktale today.
3. Do you think Soka deserved such a punishment?

"There is a strong belief among the Tumbuka that if parents are not happy with a child, the child does not find luck in whatever he or she does"

CHAPTER EIGHT

Tricksters

"Look I have found a bag, it's my bag", said Kalulu the hare.
"Don't you see that I am the one pulling it?" answered the tortoise.

INTRODUCTION

A trickster is usually of inferior size and strength but superior in cleverness. In Tumbuka folklore the tricksters are mainly the hare and tortoise. However, in some selected folktales spider is also depicted as a trickster. It is, however, very clear that the most prominent of all is Kalulu the hare.

Both folktales in this chapter have several themes but they have been grouped here to exemplify the trickery of tricksters in Tumbuka folktales.

1
KALULU THE HARE AND THE WILD DOG

Once upon a time, there was hunger in a village so Kalulu the hare and the wild dog agreed to look for food. In a nearby village however, there was one person who had a very big garden of red beans so the two decided to visit the garden and steal some of the beans.

They agreed that they would cook right there so they carried their big cooking pot. When they arrived at the garden they made a fire and started cooking the red beans.

"I will be collecting firewood while you will be adding the wood to the fire", said Kalulu the hare smiling.

Well, the two agreed. Kalulu the hare would collect firewood and the wild dog would stay in the garden cooking the beans. When the beans were about to be ready, Kalulu the hare went to the nearby river, skinned himself, put his skin in the river and then walked up to the garden while singing, *cheche chechelekete che chechelekete, cheche chechelekete che chechelekete.*

Upon seeing a strange animal singing a scary tune, the wild dog ran away for his dear life and hid himself. Kalulu the hare was very happy so he ate all the red beans on his own. Afterwards he went back to the river, put on his skin and left for the garden while carrying a few logs of wood.

"Where are you friend?" he asked.

Panting with fear the wild dog came around and shouted,

"A strange animal came here and has eaten all our beans".
"You must be very stupid, how would you let a strange animal eat our beans?" replied Kalulu the hare angrily.

The wild dog apologised to his friend so they agreed that this would not happen again. So they collected all their cooking utensils and left for home. The wild dog looked miserable and hungry.

The next day, they went again to the garden and yet again the wild dog remained in the garden while Kalulu the hare collected firewood. When the beans were about to be ready, Kalulu the hare went to the nearby river, skinned himself, put his skin in the river and then walked up to the garden while singing, *cheche chechelekete che chechelekete, cheche chechelekete che chechelekete.*

Upon seeing a strange animal singing a scary tune, the wild dog ran away for his dear life and hid himself once more. Kalulu the hare was very happy so he ate all the red beans on his own again. Afterwards he went back to the river, put on his skin and left for the garden carrying a few logs of wood.

"Where are you friend?" he asked.

Panting with fear the wild dog came around and shouted,

"A strange animal came here and has eaten all our beans".
"You must be very stupid, how would you let a strange animal eat our beans?" replied the irate Kalulu the hare.

The wild dog apologised to his friend again. And they left for home. But something bothered the wild dog. He suspected that probably his friend was playing tricks on him.

The next day they set out yet again for the garden. Each one of them attended to their prescribed activities as usual. When the relish was about to be ready as expected, Kalulu the hare left for the river and skinned himself as usual. The wild dog who had decided to secretly follow him this time around saw everything. He saw him go up the garden singing: *cheche chechelekete che chechelekete, cheche chechelekete che chechelekete.* So he went to the river and removed Kalulu the hare's skin from the water and left it to dry in the sun. When Kalulu the hare had finished eating all the beans, he came to the river and looked for his skin but found that the skin had dried up. He tried to wear it but it failed to fit him until the wild dog found him struggling to fit in the skin. Expectedly this ruined their friendship.

Questions

1. How is the hare depicted as a trickster in this folktale?
2. Discuss as many situations as possible when people trick each other in your society.
3. Dramatise the story.

2
KALULU THE HARE AND TORTOISE

Once upon a time, there was hunger in the world. So tortoise decided to beg food from people. But whenever he was given food, he would fail to carry it all because of his size. So he decided to tie a very big woven bag to his head and moved with it. Whenever he walked the woven bag followed him at the back.

One day, hare followed him.

> "Look I have found a bag, it's my bag", said Kalulu the hare.
> Don't you see that I am the one pulling it?" answered the tortoise.

After quarrelling for a long time, they decided to go to the elders for judgment. Upon listening carefully from each one of them the elders unanimously ruled that since the bag was in Kalulu the hare's hands it must have been his. So they gave all the food to Kalulu the hare. Obviously the tortoise was very angry.

One other day, Kalulu the hare was moving towards the bush to look for food. Tortoise who was still angry with the decision elders had made concerning his food saw him. This was his time to trick Kalulu the hare, he thought. So, he walked slowly towards Kalulu the hare and firmly got hold of his tail.

> "Look I have found a tail, it's my tail", said the tortoise.
> "Don't you see that I am the one pulling it?" answered Kalulu the hare.

After quarrelling for along time, they decided to go to the elders for judgment. Upon listening carefully from each one of them, the elders unanimously ruled that since the tail was in tortoise's hands it must have been his. So they cut Kalulu the hare's tail and gave it to tortoise.

Questions

1. Explain how Kalulu the hare and tortoise tricked each other in this folktale?
2. Using library information or the internet, find tricksters in:
   (a) West African folklore
   (b) East African folklore
3. What do you think is the moral of the folktale?

Reference

Cuddon, J. A. (1991). *Dictionary of literary terms and literary Theory*. London: Penguin Books Ltd.

Singano, E., & Roscoe, A. A. (1974). *Tales of old Malaŵi*. Limbe: Montfort Press.

Suggested/Further Reading

For those of you who have found Tumbuka folktales interesting, the following texts may assist in deepening your appreciation of Africa's huge oral literary heritage:

Collection of Folktales

Dicks, I. D. (2006). *Wisdom of the Yawo people: Yawo proverbs and stories*. Blantyre: CLAIM, Kachere Books no. 23.

Finnegan, R. (1966). *Limba stories and story telling*. London: Oxford University Press

Jordan, Z. P. (1973) *Tales from southern Africa*. Berkeley: University of California Press.

Mbiti, J. S. (1966). *Akamba stories*. Oxford: Clarendon Press.

Schoffeleers, J. M., & Roscoe, A.A. (1985). *Land of fire: Oral literature from Malaŵi*. Limbe: Popular Publications.

Singano, E., & Roscoe, A. A. (1974). *Tales of old Malaŵi*. Limbe: Montfort Press.

Soko, B. J. (1994). *Contes et legendes du Malaŵi*. Zomba: University of Malaŵi.

Critical Studies

Chimombo, S. (1988). *Malaŵian oral literature: The aesthetics of indigenous arts*. Zomba: Centre for Social Research.

Finnegan, R. (1970). *Oral literature in Africa*. Oxford: Clarendon Press.

Lord, A. (1964). *The singer of tales*. Oxford: Clarendon Press.

Ngwabi, B. (2002). *Oral literature in southern Africa*. Windhoek: UNESCO.

APPENDIX
Model Lesson Plan

A: PRELIMINARY INFORMATION

Class: Form 2N   **Subject:** Oral Literature
Date: 7 July 2005   **Number of Students:** 55
Time: (45 minutes) 7.30–8.15am
Topic: Oral narrative (Tasty Eggs)

B: GENERAL OBJECTIVE

Students should know and appreciate folklore.

C: SPECIFIC OBJECTIVES

By the end of this lesson students will be able to:

- identify characters in the folktale (Tasty Eggs)
- explain theme/s in the folktale (Tasty Eggs)
- discuss the relevance of the folktale (Tasty Eggs).

D: TEACHING METHODS

- Question and answer
- Whole class discussion

E: TEACHING AIDS

- A drawing of a big snake resting on its eggs in a bush.
- Shawa, L. B., & Soko, B. (2005). *Folktales from the people.* Mzuzu: Tate Publishing Company. (pp. 10–15)

F: PRESENTATION

Teacher's Activities	Students' activities
Introduction (5 minutes) • Revision of the last lesson – " A trickster narrative" • Asks students the name of the trickster in the last lesson • Asks students who the trickster tricked in the last lesson • Mentions that students will listen to another narrative "Tasty Eggs" in this lesson	• Listen to the introduction • Answer questions
Step 1 (5 minutes) • Writes the heading of the narrative "Tasty Eggs" on the chalkboard • Shows students the drawing of a snake resting on its eggs in the bush and asks them to describe what they see	• Write down the heading of the narrative in their note books • Describe what they see
Step 2 (15 minutes) • Reads the narrative " Tasty Eggs" to the class • Initiates whole class discussion by asking students to explain theme/s in the folktale	• Listen carefully • Take notes • Discuss theme/s in the folktale
Step 3 (10 minutes) Asks the following specific questions • Who are the characters in this story? • Describe how the hunters collected eggs from the snake • What mistake did the woman in the story do? • What lessons can we learn from this narrative?	• Answer questions
Conclusion (10 minutes) • Asks students to retell the narrative • Clarifies the theme/s, characters and relevance • Gives the following home work to students: *Create and write a similar folktale for class discussion during the next lesson*	• Selected students retell the narrative • Ask questions for clarification • Copy the home work

G. SELF EVALUATION